CLARK THE SHARK
AFRAID OF THE DARK

WRITTEN BY BRUCE HALE   **ILLUSTRATED BY GUY FRANCIS**

HARPER
An Imprint of HarperCollinsPublishers

To Kirsten Murphy, for all you do for kids
—B.H.

To Ben, Kristin, Hayley, and Allyssa
—G.F.

Clark the Shark: Afraid of the Dark
Copyright © 2015 by HarperCollins Publishers
All rights reserved. Manufactured in China.
No part of this book may be used or reproduced in any manner whatsoever without
written permission except in the case of brief quotations embodied in critical articles
and reviews. For information address HarperCollins Children's Books, a division of
HarperCollins Publishers, 195 Broadway, New York, NY 10007.
www.harpercollinschildrens.com

Library of Congress Cataloging-in-Publication Data
Hale, Bruce.
  Clark the Shark: afraid of the dark / written by Bruce Hale ; illustrated by Guy
Francis. — First edition.
    pages cm
  Summary: At a sleepover, Clark the Shark braves his fear of the dark with the help of
music and friends.
  ISBN 978-0-06-237450-9 (hardcover)
  [1. Fear of the dark—Fiction. 2. Sleepovers—Fiction. 3. Friendship—Fiction. 4. Sharks—
Fiction. 5. Marine animals—Fiction.] I. Francis, Guy, illustrator. II. Title.
PZ7.H1295Cm 2015   2014038656
[E]—dc23   CIP
                                                                    AC

The artist used acrylic to create the illustrations for this book.
Typography by Victor Joseph Ochoa
15 16 17 18 19 SCP 10 9 8 7 6 5 4 3 2 1
❖
First Edition

Clark the Shark looked over his list. Balloons? Check. Games? Check. Snacks? Double check. Everything was ready for Clark's first big sleepover.

Everything but Clark himself.

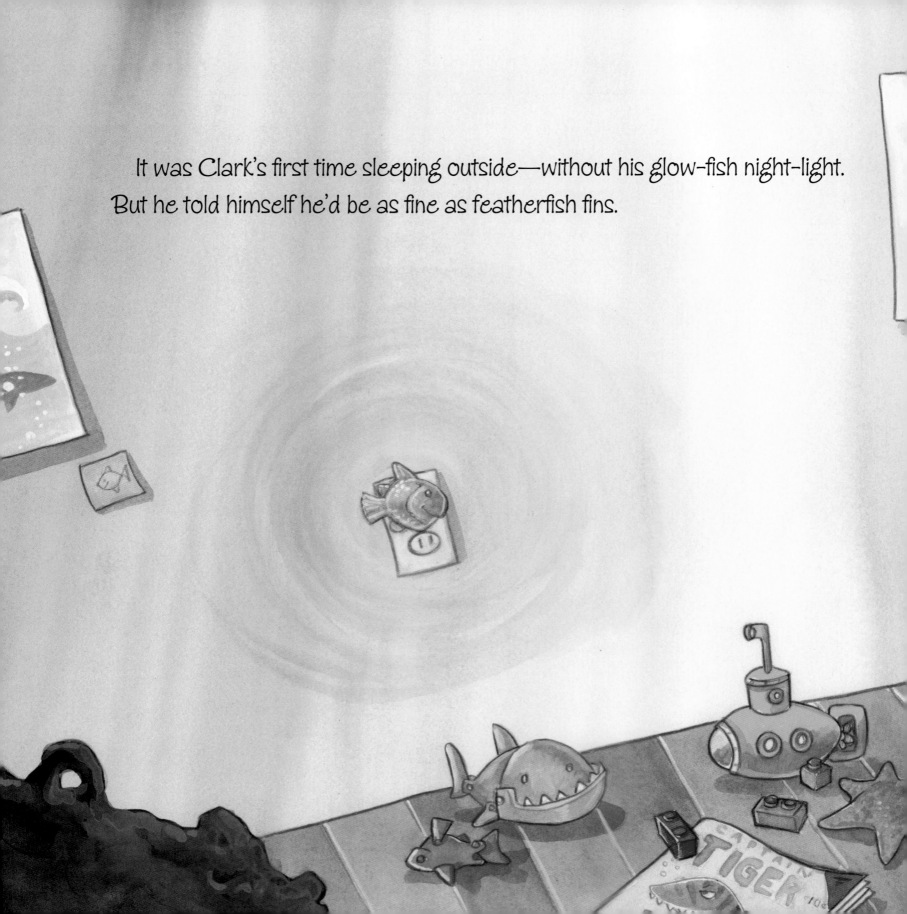

It was Clark's first time sleeping outside—without his glow-fish night-light.
But he told himself he'd be as fine as featherfish fins.

Just to be sure, Clark made a little rhyme:

"Take heart, be smart, sharks aren't afraid of the dark."

But deep down, he wasn't sure at all.

The sun sank low. The shadows stretched. Here came his friends—brave fishes, every one. Clark decided to keep his sharky mouth shut, because if they weren't afraid, then neither was he.

Clark and his friends played Hula-Hoops,
and Clark was the hoopiest of all.
"HEE-HEE-HEE, LOOK AT ME!" he cried.

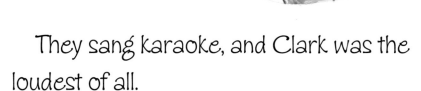

They sang karaoke, and Clark was the
loudest of all.
"LA, LA, LA, LAAA!"

They played Freeze Dance,
and Clark was the wildest of all.
Bink-bonk-ba-DONK!

"Too much sugar?" Clark's mother wondered.

Finally, she sent everyone outside. It was dark; it was scary.

To keep up his courage, Clark whispered his little rhyme:

"Take heart, be smart, sharks aren't afraid of the dark."
He didn't want to be the only one who got spooked.

"Let's tell ghost stories!" said Benny Blowfish.
Everyone looked at one another. They weren't
afraid—not them.

They told the tale of the one-eyed sea monster,

and the crazy sailor,

and the hook-handed octopus.

By the time they finished, everyone was shivery.

"Something moved over there!" cried Amanda Eelwiggle. "The crazy sailor!"
"Aaaugh!" everyone screamed.

"It's only driftwood," said Joey Mackerel.
Clark tried to relax. Then . . .

"Settle down and go to sleep," said Clark's mother, "or I'm calling your parents."

"NOOO!" cried Clark. "We'll be good."

Everyone tried to relax.

"I wasn't scared," said Kenny.

"Me neither," said Clark.

"Us neither," said everyone else.

But no one could sleep. Then . . .

"I felt a ripple," cried Joey. "Something's coming!"

"AAAUGH!" everyone screamed.

"The hook-handed octopus!"

But it was only a clump of seaweed.

"I wasn't scared," said Joey.

"Me neither," said Clark.

"Us neither," said everyone else.

The friends decided to sleep in a circle—not to be safer, just to be cozier. It was dark; it was spooky. The night was full of sounds. So Clark whispered his little rhyme:

"Take heart, be smart, sharks aren't afraid of the dark."

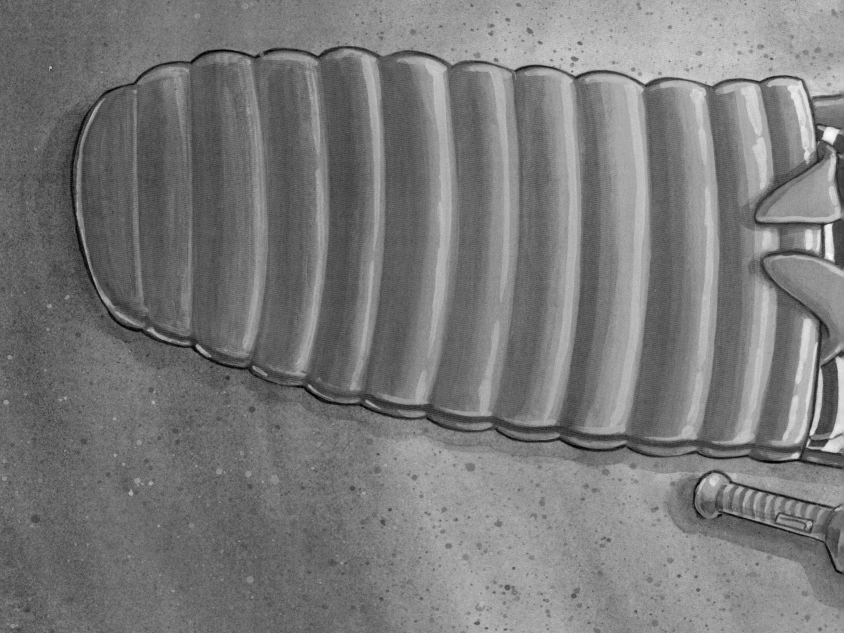

"What'd you say?" asked Joey.
"Oh, just a little rhyme," said Clark.

Joey gulped. "Are you afraid of the dark?"

Clark bit his lip. Would Joey make fun of him? In a very, very small voice,
Clark whispered, "Just a little bit."

"Me too," whispered Joey.
"Us too," whispered everyone else.

"So how do we be not afraid?" asked Joey.

Everyone thought hard, and then Clark got a big idea in his sharky head. "Let's all MAKE UP A RHYME TOGETHER!"

"Brilliant!" said Benny Blowfish. "Can we put it to *music*?"

So they did. And when they finished, everyone sang:

"Take heart, be smart, don't be afraid of the dark.
No fear, it's clear, fear is the scariest part.
Remind your mind, kick out the fear from the start.
You'll find you're fine, you're not afraid of the dark.
No, we're not afraid of the dark!"

One by one, they fell asleep humming the tune—
Clark last of all. And as they dreamed brave dreams,
the moon smiled down through the depths of the
night ocean.